The Voyageur's Paddle

Written by Kathy-jo Wargin *and Illustrated by* David Geister

To James R. Kelly, for inspiring the desire to explore and the courage to dream.

KATHY-JO

∽⚭∼

*To the teachers and librarians who nurtured my love of art and history,
and to my dear wife, Pat Bauer, who carries on that noble tradition.*

DAVID

ILLUSTRATOR'S ACKNOWLEDGMENTS

*Thanks to my friends, Mike Meyers, Susan Lieb, Tim Marino, and Spencer Johnson,
the models who helped bring life to my paintings.*

*I greatly appreciate the historical expertise of Patrick Schifferdecker, Mary Vanderpoel, and
Aaron Novodvorsky of the Minnesota Historical Society. My work at Historic Fort Snelling, as well
as research trips to the North West Company Fur Post, Grand Portage National Monument, and
Old Fort William, have all provided a vivid sketch of life in the Upper Great Lakes fur trade.*

Text Copyright © 2007 Kathy-jo Wargin
Illustration Copyright © 2007 David Geister

Sleeping Bear Press
315 E. Eisenhower Pkwy., Suite 200
Ann Arbor, MI 48108
www.sleepingbearpress.com

Sleeping Bear Press is an imprint of Gale,
a part of Cengage Learning.

10 9 8 7 6 5 4 3 2

Printed by China Translation & Printing Services Limited,
Guangdong Province, China. 2nd printing. 06/2010

Library of Congress Cataloging-in-Publication Data

Wargin, Kathy-jo.
The voyageur's paddle / by Kathy-jo Wargin ;
illustrated by David Geister.
p. cm.
Summary: Follow the yearly cycle of the voyageur Edouard as he travels
to Grand Portage, trading furs for goods that he uses to purchase more
furs during the winter months from the native villages.

ISBN: 978-1-58536-007-9

[1. Fur traders—Fiction. 2. Family life—Superior, Lake, Region—
Fiction. 3. Superior, Lake, Region—History—18th century—Fiction.]
I. Geister, David, ill. II. Title.
PZ7.W234Vo 2007
[Fic]—dc22   2006026585

About The Voyageur's Paddle

The strength and courage of the voyageurs who traveled through the Great Lakes region is legendary. With one swift stroke of their paddle, they established trading posts through the north woods territory, and many of these small posts later became towns and villages. They came in search of rich fur bearing animals, such as the beaver. Beaver skins were desired in France for the production of beaver-felt hats, which were in high demand. Voyageurs and the trading companies they worked for were an important part of opening up this vast area for commerce. However, it was their individual exploits as explorers and adventurers that captured our imaginations for decades. Their endurance seems mythical, their love of song and dance irresistible. May the pathways of the voyageurs remind us of the vibrant history of the Great Lakes, and may the spirit of the North live on in us all.

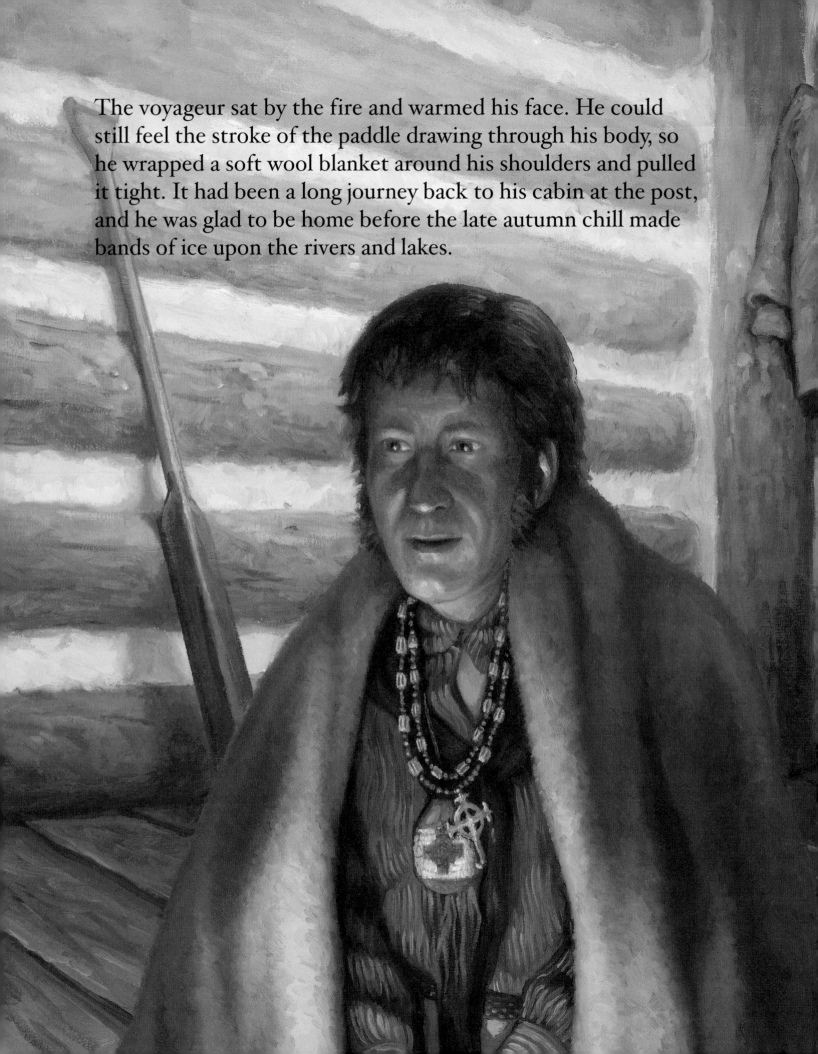

The voyageur sat by the fire and warmed his face. He could still feel the stroke of the paddle drawing through his body, so he wrapped a soft wool blanket around his shoulders and pulled it tight. It had been a long journey back to his cabin at the post, and he was glad to be home before the late autumn chill made bands of ice upon the rivers and lakes.

His name was Edouard, and he was softly singing his favorite paddling song, hoping his son, Jacques, and wife, Marie, would hear him.

One red paddle, swift and light
in the water lifting bright.
True love waits upon the shore,
and calls me home forevermore.

Marie was an Ojibwe Indian. When Edouard first came to the interior, her family helped him find new streams when old ones went dry, and told him of better paths through the forest. They showed him how to mend his canoe with sap and spruce root so that it would be strong and light, the way a north country canoe should be.

On quiet nights Marie danced while Edouard played the fiddle. The music was bright and quick, and Marie's feet made soft pattering sounds upon the wood floor. Her long black braids swinging through the air, she always called for Jacques to join her.

The trading post tucked in the north woods was the only home Jacques had ever known. Inside the palisade was a company store for trading, and other log houses like theirs, too. Each home was neat and simple, with one window and a small door.

On trading days, Jacques would ask the company clerk for permission to enter the store. Here, native people and free trappers brought hides to exchange for goods they needed, such as guns and boots, tobacco and kettles, and axes and cloth.

Sometimes Jacques helped count hides, and never made a mistake when he did. Two beaver hides for a lace cap, three hides for a good ax, and one hide for a colorful feather plume.

Jacques liked being near the other voyageurs, and he would often sing as loud as he could.

One red paddle, swift and light
in the water lifting bright.
True love waits upon the shore,
and calls me home forevermore.

Now that his father and the others were home, Jacques knew the longest part of winter was soon to follow. When the snow was deep enough, the men would depart with dog sleighs, traveling into the woods where native people had furs to trade.

The voyageurs would be gone for months, and upon their return, they
would begin preparing their canoes for the spring journey to Grand
Portage. It was far away, and the canoes must be in good shape to reach
Grand Portage by mid-summer. Jacques knew the journey was long
and dangerous, but even so, he wanted to go, too.

As Edouard worked, Jacques held his father's paddle in his hands. He wanted to be a voyageur more than anything. Gathering his courage, he asked his father if he was ready to be a voyageur just like him.

Edouard looked at his son, who still seemed small and tender. "Not yet, my son, but soon." And then went back to work.

The next morning before sunrise, Jacques stood on shore to watch his father leave. Stroke after stroke, the bright red paddle dipped into the water and slipped out of sight.

At the same time, across the Great Lakes, other brigades were leaving from Montreal with items for trading such as flour and cloth. These voyageurs were traveling west to Grand Portage in long canoes made for the freshwater sea. These men were strong and brave, but even so, they worried when the open water grew dark and angry. When the tallest waves fought against them, they tossed beads into the water for good luck and safe passage.

At the gathering, Jacques's father exchanged the furs for items to bring to the interior, while the Montreal voyageurs exchanged their goods for the furs. At night, there was lively music and celebrating outside the palisade. This was the way it was every year at the rendezvous. But this year, as everyone danced, Edouard sat upon his blanket and thought about home.

The next morning, before the bright cap of the sun broke into the sky, the men began their long journey home. They paddled during daylight, and spent nights sleeping along the rocky shores of rivers and lakes. They paddled through high summer and into early fall, their spirited voices carrying through the air as they sang their songs, dipping and pulling their way home.

Not long into their journey, Edouard began to sense something was not right. The air was turning cold faster than usual, and the lakes and rivers seemed angry and harsh. Strong waves were pushing against them, making dents and cracks in their canoes. Edouard grew heavy with worry. He paddled hard, singing with each stroke.

One red paddle, swift and light
in the water lifting bright.
True love waits upon the shore,
and calls me home forevermore.

The days were getting shorter and darker, and frost dressed the reeds in brittle white coats each night. Ice grew like fingers from the edges of the lake, and the waterways were becoming frozen, making it hard for the men to travel.

One morning with a storm approaching and the sky still dark as night, the men realized they were off course. The wind blew and the snow fell, and they looked and listened for signs to put them in the right direction.

At the post, Jacques waited anxiously. Each day he watched from shore, but saw no sign of his father or the other voyageurs. He knew they must make it home soon, or they would perish in the frozen wilderness.

That night, Jacques's mother pulled him close and said, "Your father is not home yet, Jacques, and we must prepare for a long hard winter—alone. Our hearts are heavy, but there is nothing we can do."

Seeing the tears fall from his mother's face, Jacques ran out of the cabin and to the lake. As snowflakes fell from the sky, he began to sing.

One red paddle, swift and light
in the water lifting bright.
True love waits upon the shore,
and calls me home forevermore.

Jacques sang loud, his voice pushing through the
cold night air. As the snow kept falling, he kept
singing. He sang louder and cried harder than ever
before, hoping his father would come home.

He sang and cried for hours, until his mother found
him asleep on the snow, and carried him home to bed.

That night, Jacques didn't hear the wind rush through the cabin when the door was unexpectedly opened wide. He didn't hear the heavy boots walk across the wood floor, or his mother crying and laughing at the same time.

Edouard looked at his son. Somehow as he lay sleeping, Jacques looked older and stronger to him. Edouard held his paddle in his hands, and knowing that his son had led him home, laid it gently upon his boy's bed and whispered,

"You are a voyageur now, my son, you are indeed a voyageur now."

The next morning, Edouard sat by the fire and warmed his face. Jacques sat beside him, holding the paddle tightly in his hands. For years after, he paddled the waterways with strength and courage like his father. Across lakes and rivers he went, and with his father's paddle he was always strong, he was always brave, and he was always singing his favorite song.

One red paddle, swift and light
*   in the water lifting bright.*
True love waits upon the shore,
*   and calls me home forevermore.*

New Words to Learn

Avant: the person in the front of the canoe, usually the most experienced paddler

Brigade: a group of canoes traveling together

Bourgeois: a gentleman from the trading company

Coureur de bois or **"woods runner":** an explorer who lived in the north woods and was an independent trader

en Derouine: a winter journey to Indian camps to collect furs

Engagé: an employee of a trading company

Gouvernail: the steersman, sits in the back of the canoe

Métis: someone of mixed French Canadian and Native American descent

Milieux: the person who sits in the middle of the canoe

Pays d'en haut: the north country, north and west of Lake Superior

Pose: a rest stop while portaging, usually every half mile

Rendezvous: the "great gathering," a mid-summer event at a trading post where traders exchanged furs for goods brought from Montreal

Voyageur: a person employed to paddle canoes and carry goods and furs to and from trading posts